PUZZLE JOURNEY
THROUGH TIME

Rebecca Heddle

Illustrated by Annabel Spenceley

Designed by Kim Blundell and Amanda Barlow

Edited by Jenny Tyler

History consultant: Anne Millard BA, PhD
Series editor: Gaby Waters
Cover design: Ian Cleaver

Dear reader,

Prior Place, Giddyham.

This book tells the story of the incredible adventure Lou and Matt had last year. They are my niece and nephew, and they come to stay here every summer. The house is so untidy, you can never find what you're looking for. You usually find something else instead ~ that's how the adventure started.

Sometimes, Matt and Lou got confused. They had to puzzle out what to do. Can you solve the puzzles too?

Good luck ~ Hattie Quirk

P.S. The answers are at the back.

Last summer, when Matt and Lou were staying with their Aunt Hattie, she lost her photograph album. It was full of strange old pictures. So when their aunt went out, they decided to find it for her. "It'll be more fun than playing marbles," said Lou.

In the attic

The attic was huge, and full of junk. They stared at the chaos in dismay. The album could be anywhere. Matt stumbled as he stepped off the ladder.

"Oh no," he groaned. "There goes a marble. Now we'll have to find that, too."

Matt spied his marble under a table. It was next to an unusual little box.

Matt picked up the box and rattled it at Lou. "It's quite heavy," he said.

It was full of odd things. Matt put in his marble, and picked out a coin.

"Heads or tails?" he asked, as he flipped the coin.

The coin shone brightly as it flew into the air. Lou watched it spinning in the dusty sunlight.

She had a funny feeling in her stomach, as if she were whizzing around on a merry-go-round. Matt looked rather pale, too.

3

The Viking village

The feeling passed as Matt caught the coin. But now they were surrounded by noise, as if someone had turned on a radio. Peculiar smells wafted past. Even their clothes were different. But Matt still had the box from Aunt Hattie's attic.

Where did these clothes come from?

What's happened? This isn't the attic.

"Where are we?" asked Matt. Lou peeped out from under the table and blinked in disbelief.

The room was full of people wearing funny clothes. They were eating, drinking and singing.

As Lou stood up, a bone bounced off her head. She heard voices behind her, and turned in surprise.

Go and get Harald, you two. He's going to miss Leif's speech.

You know his house. He's got hens everywhere.

They need proper directions. Go down to the sea and turn left by the ship. Turn right toward the pond, then right again by the sheep pen. That'll get you there.

Lou dragged Matt outside. "Look at that ship," he said, clutching the box. "It's like the Viking one we made at school."

"Vikings!" said Lou. "I think we should find Harald, whoever he is, and ask him some questions."

Can you see which house is Harald's?

In Harald's house

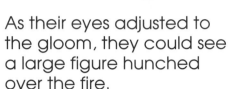

In a few minutes, they were outside Harald's house. The door opened as Matt knocked on it.

As their eyes adjusted to the gloom, they could see a large figure hunched over the fire.

He stood up and towered over the children. Lou hurriedly babbled some questions.

Harald stared at them, baffled and amused. "Am I a Viking? What sort of question is that?" he chuckled.

"And I know Leif Ericsson has been away for years, but you must have heard of him." He launched into a long story.

Leif is a relative of mine.

He lives in Greenland, so we haven't seen him for years.

He's quite an explorer. A few years back, he discovered a new land, west of Greenland.

He found vines growing there. So he called it Vinland.

But the locals are quite fierce, so no one has settled there for long.

He's going to tell us about his travels after the feast. I must go back.

He left the house, muttering, "Am I a Viking? Silliest thing I ever heard..."

Matt sat down on a bench. "I think they really are Vikings," he said.

He picked up Harald's carving, and accidentally knocked Aunt Hattie's box off the bench. Its contents scattered over the floor.

They started putting things back in the box. Matt saw some paper wedged in the bottom. "It looks like a letter," he said. It tore as he pulled it out.

Lou laid the pieces on the floor. They could still read the letter. It seemed to be written to their Aunt Hattie.

"It's about time travel," she gasped, picking up a last coin. "Is that what we've done?"

"Let's try it and see," said Matt. He took a carved green stone from the box.

Can you read the letter?

"Hattie, my dearest
This box and the
help you travel through
catch any object in h
take you to the time
came from.
You will under
ak every langu
will also cha
careful not to
you could be trapp
spe
clothes
Be
t,

child,
things in it will
time. Throw and
ere, and it will
and place that it
stand and be able to
ge you may hear. Y
ge to fit in
se this box
d in another
Your loving Father.

without
time forever

7

A fireworks party

Matt threw the stone. They felt dizzy. Then it went dark. It worked!

The air was warm and scented now. Voices were approaching, and a light.

They shrank behind a bush to listen. What were the voices discussing?

Slowly, the speakers came closer. Now Matt could see they were two women, carrying a lantern.

Lou was intrigued by the conversation. "Let's follow them. We might find out more," she whispered.

They fell into step behind the women. "All right," hissed Matt. "But where are we - and when?"

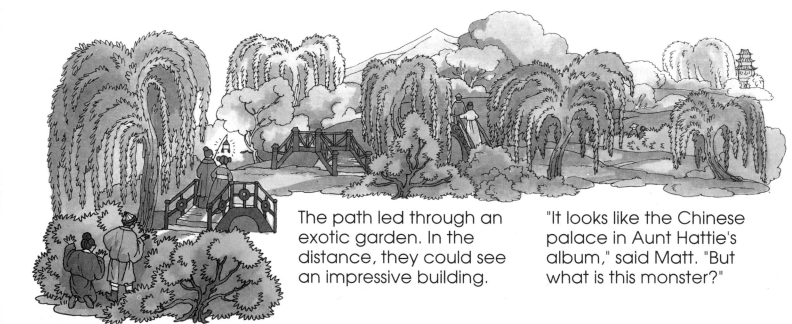

The path led through an exotic garden. In the distance, they could see an impressive building.

"It looks like the Chinese palace in Aunt Hattie's album," said Matt. "But what is this monster?"

A crowd gathered in front of the building. They hushed as a giraffe was led past. A voice announced, "This fabulous animal has been sent to our Emperor from Africa."

Lou was astonished. "It's not a monster at all! They can't have seen a giraffe before. How long ago is this?"

"I don't know," said Matt. "But there aren't any cars or electric lights."

"That's odd, I'm sure I saw a..." said Lou. Her words were drowned out by the bang of fireworks exploding.

Matt watched the display. He remembered that fireworks were an old Chinese invention. But Lou was puzzled. She fingered the coin she had picked up in Harald's house.

Lou saw something that didn't belong. Can you see what it was?

9

When in Rome

Lou dropped the coin and caught it. At once, she and Matt were in a busy street.

A hand gripped Matt by the shoulder. He tried to pull away, but it held on harder.

"Take these dormice to the kitchen," the man said. "You young slaves should be working."

He hurried them along the street. The scene around them looked like a picture of Ancient Rome, even down to the people in tunics and sandals. "So now we're Roman slaves," exclaimed Lou.

Soon they arrived at a palace. Matt and Lou were sent to the kitchen and set to work. They listened to the other slaves gossiping, and found out that they were preparing dinner for the Emperor Caligula and eight guests.

Flavia looks silly in her blonde wigs, but Petronius can't leave her alone.

Well, Julius is old enough to be Cornelia's father.

I love that brooch Livia wears. It's always on her left shoulder.

Incitatus* is coming. He'll be late, as usual.

Servius is back from Syria. He'll be so suntanned!

That's the sauce ready for the dormice.

Marcus is a mess. His clothes are awful, and his sandals are falling apart.

A few hours later, they went to take the guests' cloaks as they arrived. Matt remembered the gossip from the kitchen. He could tell who was who.

But soon he was worried. "That one's an impostor," he hissed. "She doesn't fit any of the descriptions."

Who is he talking about?

*say "In-sit-ah-tus".

11

Dinner with the Emperor

Lou and Matt were told to serve at the banquet. It was a strange affair. All the guests lay down around the table, and they picked up the food and ate with their fingers.

"We'd never get away with manners like that at home," muttered Matt.

Incitatus, my dear! So glad you could make it!

The guests were happily eating dormice and other weird dishes when a man brought in a horse. The Emperor rushed over, and greeted the horse.

"Incitatus is a horse!" giggled Lou. "Is this a joke?" But none of the diners even looked up.

The other guests greeted Incitatus, as he wandered around the room. Matt and Lou dashed around, passing plates and pouring wine.

Meanwhile, the Emperor settled down to chat with the guest they thought was an impostor. As Lou was topping up their wine, she heard something that made her blood run cold.

Have him murdered. It's sure to work.

Lou was so shocked, she didn't hear the horse come up behind her.

It nudged into her. Not thinking, she sharply pushed its head away.

Then she dropped the jug. Wine spilled all over the Emperor's feet.

Matt! Help!

"Guards!" he shrieked. "Take this slave away and kill her! She has dropped wine on me and insulted Senator Incitatus!"

Lou yelled, "Get the box! We must move on!" But Matt had put the box in a safe place, and he couldn't remember where.

Can you see the box?

Early days

Matt hurriedly threw Lou a flint from the box. At once, they escaped through time.

Now they were in a quiet, snowy landscape. As soon as Lou saw their clothes, she started to laugh.

Their Roman tunics had been replaced by smelly skins, sewn together with leather thongs.

A woman appeared from a cave behind them. She asked them to come in.

Inside, people were sitting around a fire, eating. An old man was telling stories.

After a few minutes, Matt noticed some men taking lamps and going out into the snow. "Where are they going?" he murmured, curiously.

He and Lou followed them silently out of the cave, and through the snowy woods.

The men disappeared into an opening in the hillside. The children followed them into a cave with fantastic paintings of animals on the walls. The men stood on tree trunks to work on the pictures.

But then one of the men noticed them. "You know you shouldn't be here," he said. "These paintings are sacred to our clan. Go now and I won't tell anyone."

Lou and Matt slunk out into the snow. They tried to remember the way back to the other cave.

They soon realized they were lost. But then they saw some tracks that looked like a dog's.

"The dog must belong to the cave men," said Lou. "If we follow the tracks, they'll lead us back."

The tracks led them deep into the forest. From time to time, a wailing noise broke the silence.

Now they realized what had left the tracks. They were surrounded by a pack of wolves.

There seemed to be no way to escape.

What should they do now?

Knights on horseback

Matt's hand shook as he threw a golden brooch. Just in time...

Lou looked around. "The Middle Ages," she said. "I hope we'll be safe here."

They were surrounded by merry people, laughing and joking.

The main attraction was jousting. It drew the children like a magnet.

It was exciting and scary to watch the knights charging at each other.

Lou and Matt squeezed through the crowd to get a better view.

All of a sudden, a woman appeared out of thin air, right between the knights who were jousting.

Matt dashed forward, and tripped. He dropped the box, but ran on, too excited to notice.

As Lou ran after Matt, she heard two women. She didn't realize they were talking about the box.

The mysterious person vanished as suddenly as she had appeared. The fallen knight groaned.

He looked up, bleary-eyed, then lay down again. "What on earth is that?" he asked.

Matt saw that several things had changed.

Can you see what they are?

Around the castle

"I don't like this," gabbled Matt. "There are modern things appearing. I think that person brought them. Let's get out of here."

It was then he realized he had lost the box. They had to find it, or they would be here forever!

Now Lou understood. It must have been their box that the woman Meg picked up. She was taking it to the castle. They had to get it back, and fast.

We have to find this Meg and follow her.

When she goes into a room, we'll drop behind her.

If she leaves the box, we'll slip in and get it.

As she spoke, a cart full of people drove past. Meg was on board! Quickly, they jumped onto the cart behind it.

Now they were on their way to the castle, and the box was only just out of reach.

Once they were inside the castle wall, Lou began to worry. This wasn't going to be easy. The castle was enormous, and there were people everywhere. Worse still, most of the women were dressed like Meg.

"Look very carefully, Matt," said Lou. "We mustn't lose her."

Can you see which person is Meg?

All at sea

At last they had the box back. Lou threw an earring and they arrived in a wooden room. Outside, they could hear splashing noises. The air smelled fishy, and the floor was moving. "We're on a ship," said Matt.

To Captain Abel Tasman,

Good luck on your voyage of discovery. I hope you will find the new southern continent, and open up new trade routes. Don't forget to name the land after me.

You have probably heard tales of a pirate who appears on ships as if by magic. She steals the most valuable things and leaves strange objects that no one has ever seen. Don't let these silly stories put you off.

From Governor-General Van Diemen of the Dutch East India Company.

Matt caught a piece of paper as it fell off a desk. It was covered in scrawly foreign writing. But as he stared at it, it seemed to turn into English.

Lou read it over his shoulder. "This pirate business - it sounds like what happened at the joust."

Matt's eyes lit up. "Do you suppose it could be the same woman?"

Before they could discuss it, the door swung open and the captain stalked in.

They couldn't think how to explain, as he hauled them out of the cabin.

He shook Matt roughly. "So are you stowaways? Or spies for the pirates?"

Up on the ship's deck, the captain got a sailor to tie their hands.

They listened while the ship's crew debated what to do with them.

Soon, with land in sight, the captain made his decision.

A sailor rowed Matt and Lou ashore and helped them out of the boat, as kindly as he dared.

As he left, the sailor saw something on the beach. He wrapped it up and put it in the box.

Then he rowed away.

How can Matt and Lou free themselves?

On the wagon

Lou cut the ropes with the knife. Matt threw a bullet in the air. Instantly, they were in a covered cart, full of household junk.

Outside, a line of wagons stretched as far as Matt could see. Women were walking alongside, and farther off, men on horseback were driving cattle across the plain. "The Wild West," breathed Matt.

"Hi, I'm Jesse Applegate," said a boy, running up. He thrust a hand at Matt and pulled him down.

"How are you folks?" he added. "Do you want to play?"

Lou jumped down, and joined in the rowdy game they were playing around the wagons. She would wait to show Matt what she had found in the wagon.

Suddenly, there was a shriek from one of the wagons.

A woman was crying. "Someone has stolen my necklace. It was the only valuable thing we had."

At last Lou could show Matt the poster she had found. "Matt, look!" she whispered. "Do you recognize her? It's the impostor from the Roman banquet. She's been here."

Matt recognized her as the woman at the joust, too, and remembered the letter on the ship. "Perhaps she really will change history," he said. "We have to stop her."

He looked more closely at the poster. "Well, we know where to follow her to," he said, putting his hand in the box.

Where are they going to go?

WANTED

Fools! Do you think you can stop ME? Soon I shall be the richest woman in the universe! Next stop: Then I'll change history as I choose!

FOR BANK ROBBERY AND JAIL BREAKING

The notorious bank robber, Anna Krannism, has disappeared from her jail cell. She may be heading West on the Oregon Trail. If you see her, arrest her, and hand her over to the authorities.

REWARD

The Pharaoh's trail

Lou caught the beetle-shaped Egyptian charm. The dusty American desert vanished.

Now they were in a rocky landscape, eerily lit by the moon. They flattened themselves against a rock and listened to a voice giving orders.

> Obey me. I am more powerful than your Pharaoh.

"That must be Anna Krannism. What's she up to here?" said Matt.

> Lead me to the tomb. When we're in, reseal it and leave me to it.

> But the tomb of King Tutankhamun...

> What if we are cursed for this? The valley is sacred.

"She's bullying them into robbing a tomb," gasped Lou. "That's horrid."

> Move it, worms! Your punishment will be greatest if you fail me.

Soon the villains were moving off. "We'll follow them," said Matt.

> It must be the Valley of the Kings.

Lou and Matt trailed the threesome along a path. It went steeply down into a dry, rocky valley.

Lou tripped over a rock. A hail of sand and loose stones tumbled down in front of her.

As the villains looked around, the children ducked down behind a rock - just in time to hide.

24

When they came out, Anna Krannism and her men had gone. They followed the path to the bottom of the valley and found a maze of paths leading in every direction.

Lou took the "Wanted" poster out of the box again. She hoped it might hold another clue.

Moonlight caught the back of the poster. There was a map scribbled on it.

Lou smoothed out the poster, and they stared at it, turning it to match the scene that lay before them.

X the treasure awaits me here

shows a known tomb!

"That's funny," said Matt. "The X doesn't seem to show an actual tomb." In a flash, he realized that the X marked something beside a tomb. Now he knew where to go.

Where is Anna Krannism hiding?

Tutankhamun's tomb

A bang and a blinding flash came from behind the pile of rubble. They must be on the right track.

"After you," said Lou, looking doubtfully at the passage that was blasted down into the ground.

Then she heard footsteps behind her. But before she could warn Matt, something hit her head.

When Lou came to, her hands were tied, and she was in a small room full of golden treasure.

Matt was slumped beside her. Anna Krannism snarled at them, "You can't stop me now, fools!"

"I have the best treasures of history," she crowed. "And I've replaced them with modern things!"

She laughed loudly at their bewildered faces. "But I must leave you," she continued. "Howard Carter will open the tomb in 3000 years. I'm sure he'll find you very intriguing!"

"Howard who?" muttered Matt.

Anna Krannism laughed again. She grabbed hold of a golden statue. Then she threw a silver card in the air.

Instantly, she and the statue vanished. Now Matt and Lou were alone in the Pharaoh's tomb.

Lou wriggled behind Matt. She tugged desperately at the rope around his wrists. It came loose!

Matt untied Lou. Then he grabbed the box, saying "We've got something that will help us chase her."

He had seen it in the box when they first found it.

Can you see it on page 3?

Into the future

 In a flash, they were in a strange room full of books and treasures from all sorts of times and places. They spotted a huge chest in one corner, marked "Time Travel Kit."

Anna Krannism appeared at the other side of the room. She was brandishing a nasty-looking weapon.

Suddenly, Anna Krannism was trapped in a laser cage. Three men in silver suits rushed in, ready to arrest her.

Two of the men led Anna Krannism away. The third introduced himself to Matt and Lou. "I need your help," he said.

"I have to collect all the modern things Anna's left in history," he explained. "Did you notice anything that didn't belong?"

Back home

They told Marconi all they had seen. Then Lou threw the marble Matt had put in the box when he first found it.

In an instant, they were back in the attic, and in their own clothes. Matt looked at his watch. No time had passed.

"Lou," he said, "Did anything really happen?" As he spoke, the sailor's gift fell out of the box, still wrapped in its rag.

Matt unwrapped the gift. It was an egg, and a crack was spreading across it. He set it on the floor.

After a moment's suspense, an odd little bird struggled out of the shell. Lou laughed, "Inspector Marconi has gone to find the things that don't belong in history. Let's hope he doesn't find our little dodo - they're supposed to be extinct."

Look back through the book. Can you find all the things Anna Krannism left behind?

Aunt Hattie's history notes

When Lou and Matt found the photo album, a bundle of papers tied with a blue ribbon fell out. They were all notes on history. Some were about the places Matt and Lou had been to. They spread the papers on the floor to read them.

Upper-class Roman dinners often included bizarre dishes, like stuffed dormice, just for the sake of novelty.

The Chinese invented gunpowder, and used it for fireworks long before they made war with it. In the 1400s, they made voyages to Africa. A giraffe was sent to the Emperor as a curiosity.

King Edward III of England and his successors held famous tournaments. Many were held near Windsor Castle. Windsor is still a home of the British royal family.

The most famous wagon train to travel the Oregon Trail was called the Great Emigration, as there were over 1000 settlers. One of the people who later wrote memoirs was Jesse Applegate, who was seven when he made the journey.

1922 - The find of the century
The tomb of Tutankhamun was "lost" when another tomb was built above it. It was rediscovered by Howard Carter and Lord Carnarvon. It was broken into twice in ancient times, but very little was taken. No other tomb has been found to rival it.

A Roman historian says that the Emperor Caligula's horse, Incitatus, worked as a senator in his government. The horse was often invited to banquets, and held dinner parties himself, in his marble stable in the palace.

About 17,000 years ago, Cro-Magnon men created magnificent animal paintings in caves in central France. Some of the most spectacular paintings are at Lascaux. They were found in 1940 by 4 young men.

One of the great Norse sagas (stories of the Vikings), says that Leif Ericsson was a son of Erik the Red of Greenland. He sailed to North America (which he called Vinland), about 1000 AD. He arrived there about 400 years before Christopher Columbus.

Before Australia was discovered, people thought there must be a continent there. The Dutch East India Company sent Abel Tasman to look for it in 1642. He claimed a small island to the south of Australia, which he named Van Diemen's Land (now called Tasmania). Then he sailed around the mainland without ever seeing it. On the way, he stopped at Mauritius, the island where dodos lived.

Answers to puzzles

pages 4-5 The Viking village

Harald's house is circled in red. The route Matt and Lou must take to get there is shown in red.

pages 6-7 In Harald's house
The note says:

Hattie, my dearest child,
  This box and the things in it will help you travel through time. Throw and catch any object in here, and it will take you to the time and place that it came from.
  You will understand and be able to speak every language you may hear. Your clothes will also change to fit in.
  Be careful not to lose this box - without it, you could be trapped in another time forever.   Your loving Father.

pages 8-9
A fireworks party

Lou saw this boy using a flashlight. But Matt noticed there were no electric lights.

pages 10-11 When in Rome

This is the impostor. She is pretending to be Livia, but she is wearing her brooch on her right shoulder, not her left.

All the other guests match the slaves' descriptions. The guest who is missing is Incitatus - the slaves said he would be late.

pages 12-13
Dinner with the Emperor

The box is under the couch on the left of the picture of the big banqueting scene. It is circled in red.

pages 14-15 Early days

The only way Lou and Matt can escape from the wolves is to throw something from the box and go to another time.

pages 16-17
Knights on horseback

The chalice and cups on the table have turned into a tea set.

The jouster's helmet has turned into a motorcycle helmet.

pages 18-19
Around the castle

Meg is circled in red.

pages 20-21 All at sea

The sailor dropped his knife. They can use it to cut their ropes.

pages 22-23
On the wagon

Anna Krannism has drawn some pyramids on the Wanted poster, and written "Next stop" beside them. She has gone to Egypt.

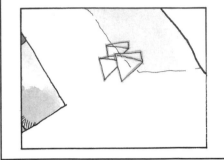

pages 24-25 The Pharaoh's trail

This is where Lou and Matt are on the map.

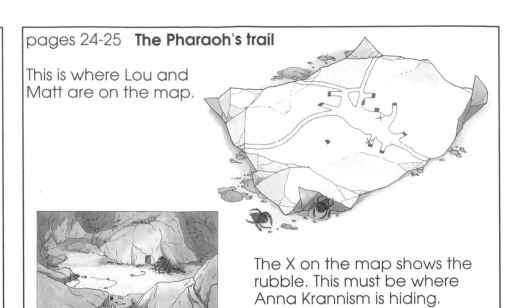

The X on the map shows the rubble. This must be where Anna Krannism is hiding.

pages 26-27
Tutankhamun's tomb

They have a silver card like the one Anna threw to leave the tomb. You can see it in the box on page 3.

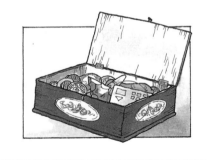

page 29 Back home
The things that Anna Krannism left behind were:

Binoculars in Harald's house.

A motorbike helmet and a tea set at the tournament.

A flashlight in China.

A personal stereo on the ship.

A pistol in Rome.

A television in the Wild West.

A tube of paint in the cave.

A mobile telephone in the tomb.

Did you notice?

Lou and Matt's grandfather appears in four of the times they visit. You can recognize him from a picture in the attic, on page 3.

First published in 1994 by Usborne Publishing Ltd, Usborne House, 83-85 Saffron Hill, London EC1N 8RT, England.

Copyright © 1994 Usborne Publishing Ltd.

The name Usborne and the device 🎈 are Trade Marks of Usborne Publishing Ltd.

Printed in Portugal.   UE